HANDBOOK OF **ATTIRE** AND **GROOMING**

The Greatest Little Book Ever On Attire And Grooming

CYRUS M GONDA

EMBASSY BOOKS

www.embassybooks.in

HANDBOOK OF ATTIRE AND GROOMING

Published in India by :
EMBASSY BOOK DISTRIBUTORS
120, Great Western Building,
Maharashtra Chamber of Commerce Lane,
Fort, Mumbai - 400 023.
Tel : (+91-22) 22819546 / 32967415
Email : info@embassybooks.in
Website: www.embassybooks.in

ISBN : 978-93-85492-21-1

INTRODUCTION

Welcome.....to what is possibly one of the 'hottest' areas of interest in the corporate world today....a crucially important sub-set of business etiquette and soft skills –

CORPORATE ATTIRE
AND GROOMING

The first impression you create when you commence your professional interaction with another person will go a long way in determining the subsequent strength of the relationship, and also have an impact on the utility and productivity of that relationship in the corporate as well as in the social context.

The manner in which you come across in terms of the effort you have taken to groom and attire yourself to project that professional touch impacts not only your first impression with the other person, but also the second, the third, the fourth, the fifth....till infinity.

You simply cannot afford to let down your 'grooming guard' for even a moment. Every single interaction you have with every single person you meet and come across is precious. Ensure that you look your very best each day as you step out of your front door in the morning – this will also ensure you function at peak levels of self-confidence throughout the day.

Clients, customers, colleagues, bosses, and even social acquaintances are increasingly more well-travelled and aware of and demanding of sartorial standards. Do not let yourself falter for even a moment on these vital parameters.

Attire yourself elegantly and groom yourself perfectly - you owe this to the organisation you represent, to your career, to your family, and most important of all, to yourself.

ACKNOWLEDGEMENTS

Almost any non-fiction book, but especially a book of this type which relies on the inputs of experienced practitioners, is a collaborative effort.

This book is no different, and would not have seen the light of day and secured space on book-shelves if it were not for the expert insights kindly offered by leading exponents from the field of corporate and social grooming and attire.

Firstly, a big thank you to **Meher Castelino** for her tips on what constitutes 'Power Dressing' in the corporate arena. There is none better qualified than her today for this job.

Ojas Rajani has literally given away all possible secrets and tips-of-the-trade with regard to hair care and skin care that must have been acquired through years of deep study. Thank you so much, Ojas.

And a big thanks to **Ashley Rebello,** who provided such specific insights, both for the areas of daily corporate attire as well as for casual dressing.

The senior faculties of the department of fashion design from I.I.T.C. (India International Trade Centre), and the head of the department, **Rina Urval,** who have all provided their knowledgeable inputs for the section on ladies' corporate attire, thank you very much.

And most important of all, a heartfelt thanks to **Vikrant Urval,** the Director of I.I.T.C., a committed educationist, an excellent human being, and a very good friend, who heads one of the best vocational training institutes in India for fashion design and travel and tourism. The students of his institute are fortunate indeed.

Lots of thanks to **Nauzad D. Irani,** who has laid out the book brilliantly, capturing the essence of the content in style.

This book would not have been possible without any of you. Thank you all very much once again
—CYRUS M. GONDA

PRACTICE THE
PRACTICAL LEARNINGS
DETAILED IN THIS BOOK AND:

- Get hold of that **'dream job'** you always wanted

- Open doors to secure appointments which you thought were out of your reach

- Have clients calling **YOU** up to give you business rather than **YOU** chasing **THEM**

- Win **MORE** sales with **LESSER** effort – Watch your sales graph zoom

- Delight your bosses, clients and colleagues

- Secure rapid promotions

- Strengthen your personal and corporate brand and relationships

- Find yourself getting accepted into the business networking group of your choice – the group you would give anything to be part of

- Watch people lining up to be in your social circle

- Rise up the corporate ladder twice as fast with half the effort

" Your elegant grooming and attire
Will set people's hearts on fire

Hair cut neat, and nails trimmed fine,
A smooth clean shave; a gentleman's shoes always shine

The rules of good grooming apply to ladies too;
Keep your nailpolish un-chipped, have a neat hair-do **"**

-CYRUS M GONDA

TABLE OF CONTENTS

Simplicity is the keynote of all true elegance

—Coco Chanel
(French fashion designer,
founder of the 'Chanel' brand)

The word 'elegant' has been defined by the Oxford Dictionary as "graceful and stylish in appearance or manner."

Isn't **'elegant'** exactly how you would like to picture yourself? Now, with the help of this book which you hold in your hands, turn the sweet vision to reality.

1 IMPORTANCE OF PROFESSIONAL **ATTIRE AND GROOMING IN A** CORPORATE ENVIRONMENT

" *When we dress professionally and formally, we make a statement that says, "I want to be* **RESPECTED,** *and I want to be* **TAKEN SERIOUSLY** "

-PROFESSOR P.M. FORNI
John Hopkins University

Dr. Judith Walters of Fairleigh Dickinson University **researched the effect of business-like appearance on the salary and compensation packages of individuals.**

She sent out two sets of almost identical resumes of potential candidates (both male and female), to more than a thousand companies. The only difference in these two sets of resumes was that one set contained resumes that were accompanied with a 'before' photo of the candidate, while the other set of resumes contained an 'after' photo of the same candidate.

'Before' and **'after'** in this case refer to a photograph with **an un-businesslike appearance** as compared to one where the same individual appears **polished, dressed in businesslike attire and is well groomed.**

Each company which received these sets of resumes was asked to determine a starting salary for the candidates.

The results were startling.

Starting salaries offered ranged from 8 to 20 percent higher for the **SAME** candidates when the 'polished' and 'business-like appearance' photos were attached to the resumes as compared to when the photos of the same persons which did not project a businesslike appearance were attached.

All else being equal, for the **same** person with the **same qualifications** and **experience**, simply being attired and groomed pleasingly and professionally made a positive difference of **8 to 20 percent in salary offered.**

Imagine, prospective customers and clients must be thinking in similar terms with regard to the attire and grooming of the salespersons and entrepreneurs they interact with as well.

PROFESSIONALS DRESS TO GET
respect and gain credibility

I f you ever visit a doctor or a dentist at their dispensary or a lawyer in his chambers or a chartered accountant in his office for the first time and you find them:

- With their hair spiked in a 'Mohawk' and dyed green

- Tattoos adorning every visible inch of their skin

- Studs and piercings on their ears and tongue

- Dressed in pink fluorescent shirts and ripped purple jeans

- Flip-flop footwear on their feet.....

......Chances are that you will say, "Sorry, I must be in the wrong place," and hurriedly head for the exit.

There is (a) difference between putting on clothes and dressing well

-WAYNE CHIRISA

It is not only doctors, dentists, lawyers, and chartered accountants who are entitled to call themselves as professionals.

Salespersons, customer service persons, entrepreneurs, key account handlers, telephone operators and receptionists – in fact any person doing any job with honesty and dignity – all have the right to proudly label themselves as 'professionals' also – so long as they possess and demonstrate relevant professional knowledge and expertise, and groom and attire themselves in a professional manner.

2 WHAT CONSTITUTES PROFESSIONAL ATTIRE

" What a strange power there is in clothing "

-ISAAC BASHEVIS SINGER

Many people believe that what constitutes professional attire differs from industry to industry.

But I disagree.

--------Strongly.

Yes, the specific outfit may differ based on the specific needs and requirements of a particular job, but that does **NOT** give license to dress shabbily and casually, and be a disgrace to the profession one represents.

For example, today in the profession of advertising, which is said to be a 'creative' profession, (which profession is **not** a creative one?), a lot of leeway in terms of formal dressing is often taken for granted and unfortunately even permitted. This is apparently nothing but an excuse by some practitioners to project themselves in a sloppy manner.

A s an interesting exercise, just take some time to view the photographs on the Internet of perfectly-attired titans from the field of advertising such as:

- **David Ogilvy** (founder of *Ogilvy & Mather* and an individual whom *Time* magazine once called 'The most sought-after wizard in today's advertising industry')

- **Leo Burnett** (founder of *Leo Burnett Company, Inc.*, one of the top-ranked creative agencies in the world even today)

- **Bill Bernbach** (Ranked 'Number One' on *Advertising Age's* '20th century honour roll of advertising's most influential people')

- **Albert Lasker** (who is considered the 'founder of modern advertising').....

......and you will immediately realise that the shabby attire you see casually draped on the frames of many advertising 'professionals' today is nothing but an outcome of sheer laziness and lethargy, and has nothing whatsoever to do with the specific demands or requirements of the advertising profession.

Even in the current Indian context, as an outstanding example, observe the way **Mr. Sam Balsara**, the founder, Chairman and Managing Director of Madison World and Madison Communication; one of the leading figures in the Indian advertising industry, grooms, attires, and carries himself. Never a hair out of place. Always impeccably attired and groomed to perfection, Sam is an outstanding example of a professionally attired individual, standing out even more so because he positively represents the otherwise 'casual' world of advertising.

Briton Hadden

Or in journalism, another profession where sloppy dressing is often currently condoned and accepted as par-for-the-course.....view the photographs of the stalwarts of journalism. Men such as **Henry Luce**, who founded the *Time, Fortune* and *Life* magazines, or **Briton Hadden**, who was *Time* magazine's first editor and the inventor of its revolutionary writing style known as 'Time-style.'

There is a reason why doctors, lawyers, accountants, are always dressed at their most professional when interacting with their patients and clients.

Their attire generates confidence among their patients and clients and clearly conveys that the individual they are dealing with is a thorough professional.

In management parlance, this is termed as the *Halo Effect*, wherein if a person meeting another for the first time observes one outstanding attribute in the other (excellent communication, impeccable attire and grooming, charming and genuine smile), the **OVERALL** first impression would be a positive one. This is because that one outstanding element overshadows everything else, and the relationship starts on the right note.

There is no reason why perfect grooming and elegant attire need be restricted to doctors and lawyers alone. **EVERY** profession, including the one **YOU** may happen to represent, would be happy to see its representatives groomed and attired at their best when they face their clients and colleagues to 'get the job done.'

Richard Nixon

Of course, if you are a rock-star, then the rules of dressing would differ, as the following hilarious but instructive anecdote reveals:

When **Richard Nixon** was the American president, the rock-icon **Elvis Presley** had been invited to the White House to stage a music performance.

Elvis as usual went attired in his trademark wild and flashy white-sequinned jumpsuit with flaring bell-bottom trousers.

When President Nixon (who was always soberly attired as befitted his status and role as president of the U.S.A.), met Elvis, Nixon commented on the outrageousness of Elvis' costume. Elvis grinned his charming, trademark, boyish grin and replied:

Elvis Presley

"Well, Mr. President..... you have YOUR show to run, and I have MINE."

SO TRUE.

President Nixon **would** have looked out of place in the White House dressed up in an Elvis Presley style rock-concert outfit, and Elvis would have looked equally out of place on a stage facing a teenage audience in a suit-and-tie combination such as Richard Nixon wore to work as the president of the U.S.A.

" *Clothes are part of the character. They can't but help inform who you are* **"**

-JILL CLAYBURGH

So what exactly **ARE** the components of professional attire?

Primarily, your attire at work should translate as –

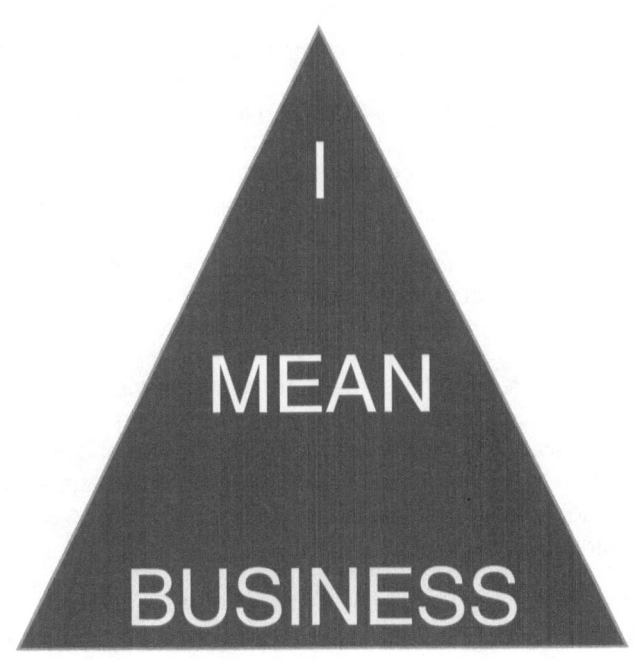

A TRUE STORY OF A RISE TO
THE TOP

> ## *If you want to rise to the top fast, you have to constantly look and act the part while still lower down and on your way up*
>
> ### -CYRUS M. GONDA

A brilliant example of the power of grooming in the sales profession is often narrated by my good friend Dr. Kalim Khan, with regard to a former MBA student of his.

After completing his course, like many other fresh MBAs, the student secured a job with the sales department of a private bank.

However, unlike many others, this lad gave great importance to getting his personal attire and grooming just right, right from day one of his career.

He made a few clothing investments the moment he started working. He got stitched for himself three well-fitting suits, purchased a few excellent ties, and two good pairs of formal shoes. Each day he came to work; he came attired in a suit. His colleagues laughed and even sometimes mocked at him, as they never wore a suit to office. He smiled and took it in his stride.

When his colleagues went for sales visits to clients' offices, they travelled by public transport and pocketed the taxi fare to which they were entitled. This lad actually went on his sales visits by taxi, using the taxi allowance the office provided. He reached his client locations on time, looking fresh, also having applied a deodorant in the taxi on the way.

Within the first two months of his being on the job, his sales volumes showed a superior performance as compared to his colleagues, who were equally qualified. **Appointments which were impossible to secure for other salespersons, were secured by him with ease**. Personal secretaries of bosses who wouldn't give a glance to the averagely groomed salesperson, willingly gave appointments to this well-groomed and attired individual.

One fine day, the sales manager of the bank had a high-level appointment with the senior management of another organisation. He wanted one of the junior staff members to accompany him.

Guess who he selected?

You're right.

Our friend.

And guess **WHY** he was the one selected?

Right again.

And all due to the attention he paid to his grooming. The icing on the cake was that in this particular client meet where his boss took him along, the clients initially felt that this lad was the boss, (due to his impeccable dress), and greeted him first. The boss was literally sidelined.

> **"*INVEST SENSIBLY IN YOUR APPEARANCE. It is one of the best professional investments you could ever make***"

-CYRUS M. GONDA

OFFICE ATTIRE – CAREFULLY CHOSEN – GIVES GREAT **'RETURN-ON-INVESTMENT'**

Therefore, if possible, you should set aside some amount of money every quarter from your salary to invest in quality attire. The **'Return-on-Investment'** would be well worth it.

Good clothes need not be very expensive, they need not be purchased from the outlets of renowned brands, but they **should** drape well and not wrinkle once worn. Good fabric is also lasting and does not wear out so easily. Once you invest in good attire, it will last you for a long time to come.

Do not shop impulsively and squander your clothing budget on something which you will later regret buying.

Rather, do your homework well by observing what the best-attired people in your organisation are wearing in terms of colour, style, design and fit. Then identify where you could get similar attire at a reasonable price. If you are not very confident of your shopping ability, take along a trusted friend who knows 'clothes' well and let him help you out.

Once you make your wardrobe purchases:

- Take care of them well

- Store them properly

- Inspect them regularly to ensure they are in good shape

- Ensure they are washed and ironed before every use

"*Dress how you want to be addressed*"

–Bianca Frazier

As far as tips and pointers on formal office attire are concerned, the following are simple, practical and evergreen pointers for corporate attire, especially in the Indian context.

"*Carelessness in dressing is moral suicide*"

-HONORE DE BALZAC

CORPORATE ATTIRE FOR GENTS

<TROUSERS>

- Ensure the material is of a polyester-blend so it does not wrinkle easily

- Trousers should preferably be in dark colours – black, brown, navy blue, grey

- Beige trousers are permissible with a dark shirt

- Wear trousers which complement your shirt, not clash with it (White shirts go with any shade of trouser)

- Brown trousers match with cream or beige shirts; blue shirts gel well with grey or black trousers. Classic combinations are always the best

- Ensure trousers fit well and are neither too tight nor too 'baggy'

- Keep trouser pockets free of anything but your handkerchief

- Ensure your belt fits well into the loops of your trousers. If the loops are too large and the belt too narrow, the loops of the trousers sag over the belt and this look untidy

- Your trousers should ideally be worn at the waist just above the hips

- At the bottom, your trousers should neither be too long so they trip you up, nor too short. The ideal trouser length should end half-an-inch from the ground when you are standing erect in your shoes

- Front creases of trousers should always be sharply ironed and cuffs (edges) at the bottom of trousers should always be clean

<SHIRTS>

"What you wear is more important than what you say, and if your shirt's not ironed, impressions are instantly formed about you"

-JAROD KINTZ

- Shirts should be of cotton fabric or of cotton-polyester blend, especially in a tropical climate such as we have throughout most of India

- Ensure the material you select is relatively wrinkle-free

- They should be full-sleeved (with the sleeves rolled down)

- Shirts should preferably be of lighter colours than the accompanying trousers

- Shirts should preferably be of solid/single colours. This is also called as bold or monotone

- Best colours for corporate shirts – white/blue/grey

- If there is some design on the shirt, the design should be small prints and not bold. No thick stripes or bold checks

- Collars of shirts should be of formal style and well-ironed

- Since in most cases you will wear shirts tucked into your trousers, the shirt should be long enough so that it stays well tucked in even when you are seated

- In case you are wearing a straight-bottomed shirt and not tucking it into your trousers but leaving it out, the length of the shirt should not exceed the lower part of your trouser's zipper

- The shirt should not be very tight but sufficiently loose to allow free movement without being uncomfortable

- You should be able to lift your arms freely in your shirt without feeling uncomfortable at the arm-pits

- The seams of the shirt at your shoulder should not droop but should just fall over your actual shoulders

- The cuff of your sleeve should lie an inch below the wrist when your sleeves are rolled down

- When wearing a tie, always ensure that the top button of your shirt is buttoned shut

- If not wearing a tie, only the top-most (collar) button should be left open. All other buttons below it should be buttoned up

- Always ensure the shirt you are wearing is neatly ironed

<SUITS / BLAZERS>

" *I can go all over the world with just three outfits: a blue blazer and gray flannel pants, a gray flannel suit, and a black tie* **"**

-PIERRE CARDIN

----------A question often asked is –

What is the difference between a suit jacket and a blazer?

The answer is – practically today, there is really not much difference between a suit jacket and a blazer except that one comes with matching pants and the other does not.

----------Another question asked is–

What is the difference between a single-breasted jacket and a double-breasted one?

The answer, according to Wikipedia, is that the term double-breasted refers to a coat or jacket with wide, overlapping front flaps and two parallel columns of buttons or snaps; by contrast, a single-breasted coat has a narrow overlap and only one column of buttons

Single-breasted

Double-breasted

Which is the more popular format of suit jacket today?

The single-breasted variety is far more common today, and it is a style which is evergreen and which suits all body shapes and types.

Should the single-breasted jacket have two or three buttons?

The two-buttoned variety is more common and in vogue, but the three-buttoned jacket suits exceptionally tall men.

Should the buttons on a suit jacket be buttoned-up or left open?

With the three-buttoned variety, always keep the bottom-button open. Ideally only the middle-button should be buttoned-up.

Even in a classic two-button suit, only close the top-button when you want the suit buttoned-up.

The bottom-button of a jacket should always be open even when you are standing.

Open all buttons on your jacket when you are seated.

The top-button of a two-button jacket or the middle-button of a three-buttoned one should ideally fall at or just above your navel.

<TIPS FOR JACKETS / SUITS>

" Like every good man, I strive for perfection, and like every ordinary man, I have found that perfection is out of reach – but the perfect suit is not out of reach "

-EDWARD TIVNAN

- Invest in at least one good quality, well-tailored suit

- Ideal colours for corporate suits are dark-navy, charcoal-grey, or tan (Avoid jet-black for suits)

- While ideally the two-piece suit should be in monotone (single colour), subtle stripes or patterns are acceptable

- The jacket length when you are standing erect should reach the tip of your thumb with your arm hanging straight down by your side

- The jacket should be sufficiently long enough to cover buttocks at the back and the trouser zipper in the front

- The jacket sleeve should be of a length to allow upto half-an-inch of shirt-sleeve cuff to show when your arm is hanging straight down

- When you are purchasing a ready-made suit, the first thing to do is to check whether the shoulders fit well

- Double-slits on the sides at the back of the jacket are more comfortable and fashionable than a single-one in the centre

" *Clothing doesn't really change a man, but it changes how others react to him* "

-BRANDON SANDERSON

Cyrus M. Gonda

CORPORATE LADIES' ATTIRE

" *The dress must follow the body of a woman, not the body following the shape of the dress* "

-Hubert de Givenchy

Expert inputs for ladies attire (both Indian and Western) have been kindly provided by **Rina Urval, Head of Department – Fashion Design** with the **India International Trade Centre (IITC)**, and **Geeta Shah** and **Khushboo Nanavati**, both being **senior faculties** in the **Department of Fashion Design with IITC.**

LADIES' CORPORATE **WESTERN** WEAR

"*The dress must not hang on the body, but follow its lines. It must accompany its wearer and when a woman smiles, the dress must smile with her*"

-MADELEINE VIONNET

GENERAL TIPS

- For Western wear (pant-suits and skirt-suits), select neutral colours such as beige, brown, navy-blue, black, and grey for jackets, skirts and slacks

- If wearing skirts to work, always team up with stockings

- For shirts or blouses, white is always a very good option, but other matching (but not loud) colours such as cream or light-blue would do as well

SKIRTS

- Skirts should be loose enough to be comfortable and of appropriate length even when seated

- No high-slitted skirts

- Skirts should fall to knee-length or just above knee-length while standing

SHIRTS/BLOUSES

- Not short-sleeved

- Conservative necklines

- No bright colours or loud patterns

- Solid whites and off-white, light blue/grey are the best colours

- Soft patterns are permitted

- Light stripes and small checks are permitted

LADIES' CORPORATE **INDIAN** WEAR

> **" Fashion can be bought. Style one must possess "**
>
> -EDNA WOOLMAN CHASE

SAREES

- Georgette, cotton or chiffon *sarees* are best

- Preferably single coloured *sarees*

- Best colour options – dull to light. Best colours for *sarees* would be blue, grey, mauve, and pastel shades

- Dark-coloured borders and blouses combine well with light/dull coloured *sarees*

- If wearing an embroidered *saree*, ensure the embroidery is only thread-work and not glittering embroidery

- *Sarees* should not be very heavy

SALWAAR-KAMEEZ

- Ideally should be of solid, single colours

- Less of prints

- If prints, then should be self or soft and small prints

> **"Your clothes should be tight enough to show you are a woman but loose enough to show you are a lady"**

-MARILYN MONROE

LADIES – WHETHER WEARING

INDIAN OR WESTERN WEAR......

AVOID

- TIGHT-FITTING CLOTHES
- SLEEVELESS ATTIRE
- PLUNGING NECKLINES

" Clothes don't make a man, but clothes have got many a man a good job "

-HERBERT HAROLD VREELAND

(And, I would add, have got many a salesman a good order as well)

Bear in mind, you do **NOT** need to be among the first to adopt a new fashion trend

FUNNY FASHION FACT

King George V

Sometimes, being too ahead of fashion can cause lighter moments – In the court of **King George V**, a courtier appeared in front of the king, attired in the latest fashion, **with the bottom cuffs of his pants turned high up, as per the latest trend of the time**.

Unaware of this very recent trend in fashion, King George commented – **'I was not aware that the floors of my palace are damp.'**

Trends come and go too fast for you to keep up with them. Investing in classic clothing is always your best bet.

To be a fashionable woman is to know yourself, know what you represent, and know what works for you. To be "in fashion" could be a disaster on 90 percent of women. Remember, you have your own identity; you are not a page out of 'Vogue' magazine

-UNKNOWN

You **CAN** and **SHOULD** look elegantly attired – **WITHOUT** having to spend a fortune

The following article appeared in the Mumbai edition of *The Times of India* (page 19) dated 3rd October, 2012.

The article was titled – '**Work Clothes Eat Up Women's Pay**' and an extract from the article follows:

'**W**omen spend 18% of their yearly income on their working wardrobe, as they feel the pressure to look good at work, a research has found. Competitive dressing in the workplace is fast increasing and women spend 18% of their salary – an average of 341 pounds a month – on their working clothes. Seven out of ten women are under pressure to dress to get noticed, found the **survey**... (a U.K. based survey)'

The point here is – Indian women (and men) today face similar pressure. The trick is to try to identify clothes and accessories that can get you positively noticed, without putting a deep hole in your pocket.

Many small boutiques and apparel shops in every city and town provide good value for money. Shop around in your city and find the right sources which offer you 'value for money' clothing.

You **CAN** look elegant **WITHOUT** spending a huge fortune.

And that brings us to...............

ASHLEY REBELLO

Ashley Rebello is known in the Indian fashion circuit as the **'MAN WITH THE GOLDEN TOUCH.'**

A man who can take the simplest and most basic of fabrics and turn them into works of art.

Ashley is the leading designer to the Bollywood stars and also many senior corporate executives.

A few of the celebrities who rely on Ashley to fashion their attire and accessories are:

- Salman Khan
- Sonakshi Sinha
- Jacqueline Fernandez
- Imran Khan
- Priti Shahani (head of Junglee Motion Pictures)
- Kiran Rao-Khan

Ashley is the **Brand Ambassador** for the **Inter National Institute of Fashion Design (INIFD), a fashion columnist for the DNA** newspaper (his column – *Designer Diaries*, appears in every Thursday or Friday edition), and he is also the proprietor of the high-end fashion store in Bandra, Mumbai – called *Ahakzai*.

Ashley was kind enough to grant me a personal interview and share his tasteful insights into the exquisite colour combinations he personally recommends for corporate wear.

Simply reading through the combinations he has suggested (for both gents and ladies), conjures up attractive images of the well-dressed corporate individual.

In one word, his combinations sound '**YUMMY.**'

Ashley believes that the **RIGHT LOOK FOR WORK** can be **achieved with relatively little investment** as long as your **choice of colours is tasteful and attractive, without appearing to be loud and overbearing**.

He mentions the following **colour combinations** as his personal favourites, and also encourages you to experiment with combinations which 'work for you.'

For **MEN AT WORK**, Ashley suggests:

COMBINATION ONE

- Dark military green trousers
- Mint-coloured shirt
- Mustard-coloured tie
- Tan shoes

COMBINATION TWO

- Charcoal-grey trousers
- Baby-pink shirt / Ice-blue shirt
- Tie matching the shirt (Tone-on-Tone)
- Black shoes

COMBINATION THREE

- Black trousers
- White shirt
- Ink-blue tie / Dark purple tie
- Black shoes

FOR
WESTERN LADIES' FORMAL WEAR,
Ashley offers the following suggestions:

COMBINATION ONE

- Chocolate brown skirt
- Lemon yellow top
- Tan shoes

COMBINATION TWO

- White pants
- Mint-coloured shirt / top
- Tan shoes

COMBINATION THREE

- Steel-grey pants / skirt
- Peach-coloured top
- Black shoes

And for LADIES' INDIAN WEAR,
Ashley recommends:

- A long ankle-length fitted *kurta* with big slits till the waist and Palazzo pants, rounding off the combination with a scarf

  (As a possible colour-combination for the above, he suggests a Biscuit-coloured *kurta* with Rose-coloured pants and a printed scarf)

  He mentions that there should be no embroidery on the *kurta* and it should ideally be in solid, single colours or it could have light stripes / small checks / self designs

For *Sarees,* Ashley recommends that for corporate wear, they should be:

- Cotton or chiffon
- Solid, single colours
- Having nice contrasting borders
- Printed three/fourth sleeve blouses

The colour combinations he suggests for *sarees* are:

ONE – Maroon *saree* with a black border

TWO – Turquoise *saree* with an emerald border

THREE – Grey *saree* with a pink border

ONCE YOU BUY YOUR CLOTHES, TAKE CARE OF THEM

A nd after all that hard work and investment in selecting and purchasing the right attire, Ashley offers some tips for taking care of your clothing:

- After preferably hand-washing your clothes, rinse them in *Comfort* fabric softener so that the clothes stay soft and last longer

- Iron and either keep your clothes folded or on hangers so you can wear them straight away when needed

- Keep combinations ready, so that no time is wasted in the morning over deliberating and deciding – 'What do I wear today?'

(Ashley adds that when he interviews trainee designers to intern with him, if they come dressed in unironed clothes, or even the samples of their work which they're carrying with them are not ironed, he rejects the candidates – even if their designs are very good.)

I am sure all the gents and ladies reading this book will benefit greatly from Ashley's inputs on the subject of formal office attire.

But this is not all. Ashley will be back in the section on **FRIDAY DRESSING** with more of his unique combinations to help you get your casual attire just right.

PEOPLE WILL OFTEN JUDGE YOU AND WHAT YOU WORK AS, BASED ON YOUR ATTIRE

" Know, first, who you are; and then attire yourself accordingly "

-EPICTETUS

Keir Hardie, a Scottish-born British politician, was one of the founders of the Labour Party.

In his early life, he had been a coal-miner and a trade-unionist.

When he was elected to the British Parliament House in 1892, he walked up to Parliament House on his first day there, dressed in his ordinary working clothes and simple cloth cap.

The policeman at the gate, looking at Hardie's attire, asked him suspiciously if he was working here.

Hardie replied, "Yes."

The policeman, assuming based on Hardie's attire that Hardie was a workman who had come to repair the building, further enquired,

"On the roof of the building?"

Hardie, the newly elected Member of Parliament, replied,

"No. On the floor of the House."

AN EXCEPTION TO THE RULE

Albert Einstein, And of course, there are some, like the genius who just **HATE** dressing up.

Once when his wife asked Einstein to change his clothes as the German Ambassador and other dignitaries were due to visit them, Einstein grumbled and said: "**If they want to see me, here I am. If they want to see my clothes, open my closet and show them my suits.**"

Once you reach the stature of Albert Einstein, perhaps you, too, could get away with such indifference to your attire. But until then.........you need to follow the rules of the game.

Of course, Einstein was correct when he remarked that along with proper attire, our minds and our hearts also need to be functioning to their full capacity. As he put it in his inimitable manner:

"**If most of us are ashamed of shabby clothes and shoddy furniture, let us be more ashamed of shabby ideas and shoddy philosophies.....it would be a sad situation if the wrapper were better than the meat wrapped inside it**"

YET ANOTHER EXCEPTION TO THE RULE

Mark Twain, though a brilliant author and a very fine human being, was always a little careless about his attire.

One day he called on the civil-right activist, Harriet Beecher Stowe. On his return home, his wife noticed he had visited the lady without having on his necktie and scolded him for this omission of dress-etiquette.

A little later, a messenger (sent by Mark Twain), turned up on Harriet Beecher Stowe's doorstep and handed her a small package. Inside the package was a note, and a black necktie.

The note read: 'Here is a necktie. Take it out and look at it. I think I stayed half an hour this morning without this necktie. At the end of that time, will you kindly return it, as it is the only one I have. Mark Twain.'

Mark Twain, being Mark Twain, could get away with this. You may not be able to.

Yet, it is Mark Twain who once humorously remarked:

"Clothes make the man.
Naked people have little or no influence in society"

ATTIRE YOURSELF APPROPRIATELY FOR THE OCCASION AND FOR THE AUDIENCE

Julia was the daughter of the Roman Emperor **Augustus Caesar**.

Once she came into her father's presence, wearing a dress which was rather immodest.

Though not happy with her choice of dress, her father did not correct or rebuke her.

The very next day, to his great pleasure, Julia appeared in a very modest dress which suited her status.

Caesar said to her, "This dress is much more suitable for the daughter of Augustus Caesar.

Julia politely replied, **"Today I dressed to meet my father's eyes, yesterday it was for my husband's."**

Cyrus M. Gonda

" **Clothes and manners do not make the man; but, when he is made, they greatly improve his appearance** "

–HENRY WARD BEECHER

YOUR EMPLOYER PAYS YOUR SALARY –HE/SHE DECIDES HOW YOU DRESS

"
What to wear: An employee chooses
How to dress: His employer chooses
"

-Mokokoma Mokhonoana

SIZZLING HOT 'ATTIRE' TIP –

If the organisation you represent has a dress code or dress policy, make sure that what you wear to work professionally fits within the framework of that dress code.

A FUNNY FACT–

While many organisations have dress code policies which run into pages: (for example, 'abc' is the attire when in office on a normal day, 'efg' should be the attire during corporate events, 'hij' is acceptable monsoon wear, 'klm' can be worn as casual dress, and so on – the **Semler Corporation** of Brazil has a very practical, simple, and unique 'Official Dress Code' for its employees. It consists of just two words:

'Dress Sensibly'

I f your organisation trusts you to dress and groom yourself well when you represent them, don't betray their trust.

Your attire should primarily look professional at all times, at least when you are 'ON THE JOB.'

Observe even a soccer or a basketball coach and the manager of a soccer or a basketball team on the sidelines when their team is playing on the field. They are always dressed like CEOs of multi-national corporations, not in track-suits or tee-shirts. That should give you a good idea as to what professional attire is all about.

General Tips For
CORPORATE ATTIRE

Clothes mean nothing until someone lives in them

-MARC JACOBS

- Your clothes at work should always be clean, well-ironed and fit you well

- Both gents as well as ladies should avoid very bright colours and large prints

- Make a quick check when you leave home and after visiting the washroom to ensure trouser zipper is up and secure

- Select the outfit you are going to wear to work the next day the evening before, just like you packed your bag for school one evening before

- If you are provided with a locker at work, always keep a clean, ironed outfit there ready for any emergencies (such as spillage on or tear in the current clothes you may be wearing)

- The clothes you wear (style/colour/cut) should suit your personality, your skin tone, and your body type well

> **" Fashion is not necessarily about labels. It's not about brands. It's about something else that comes from within you "**

-RALPH LAUREN

And ultimately, while your attire and accessories are undoubtedly important, it is good etiquette to not mention to those around you where you bought them and especially how much they cost.

Do not, for example, deliberately draw attention to the 'brand label' on your clothes and accessories. People will observe these anyway, and it is not considered good manners to initiate conversation about them.

> **" A man should look as if he had bought his clothes with intelligence, put them on with care, and then forgotten all about them "**

-HARRY AMIES

3 THE ROLE OF ACCESSORIES

> **" The only thing that separates us from the animals is our ability to accessorise "**
>
> -ROBERT HARLING

According to our trusted friend, Wikipedia, the definition of a fashion accessory is an item used to contribute, in a secondary manner, to the wearer's outfit, often used to complete an outfit and chosen to specifically complement the wearer's look. The term came into use in the 19th century.

Accessories consist of, but are not limited to:

- Shoes
- Socks
- Ties
- Belts
- Stockings
- Bags
- Purses
- Watches
- Jewellery
- Cuff links
- Tie clips
- Handkerchiefs
- Umbrellas

Shoes are probably the **most important accessory** and **should be given priority** by gents and ladies alike.

A FUNNY FASHION FACT –

High heels were first worn by **MEN**. Then in the 1600s, women started wearing heels to look more masculine, and so men stopped wearing them to avoid looking feminine.

"A great suit looks well with a good pair of shoes, you cannot separate the two"

-WAYNE CHIRISA

GUIDELINES FOR **GENTS'** SHOES

- Purely formal design, not even semi-formal

- If wearing a suit, definitely wear shoes with laces

- Even otherwise, laced shoes are considered more formal

- Shoes should be either black or brown

- No fancy designs or flashy buckles

- Ensure they are always well polished

- Avoid wearing shoes with worn-out heels, you can always get them repaired and resoled

" *Shoes are worth 10$ per compliment* "

-TERRI GUILLEMETS

AND TIPS FOR
SOCKS

- No white socks at work – ever

- Socks should match the shoe and trouser colour

- Gent's socks should reach at least till mid-calf high so the skin of your leg or calf doesn't show even when you are seated

- Change socks daily to avoid odour

"Never, ever, wear white socks at work. While some may consider business to be a game, it is certainly not a tennis match"

-CYRUS M. GONDA

GUIDELINES FOR **LADIES'** SHOES

" Give a girl the right pair of shoes and she'll conquer the world "

-MARILYN MONROE

LADIES' SHOES – **YES**

- Two to three inch heels, not more
- Match colour of shoes with attire and other accessories
- Preferably shoes should be in white, grey, black or beige colours
- Conservative design

LADIES' SHOES – **NO**

- Open-toed designs
- Sandals/Strappy sandals
- Shiny and glitzy straps or buckles
- Bright colours
- Stilettos

ALL ABOUT
TIES

n a P.G. Wodehouse novel, the character Bertie Wooster, who is obviously worried about some matter, tells his butler, Jeeves, "What do ties matter, Jeeves, at a time like this?"
Jeeves, the epitome of elegance, politely replies, "**There is no time, sir, when ties do not matter.**"

TIPS FOR **NECK-TIES**

- Conservative, sober colours are always in vogue
- Solid, single colours are preferred
- If striped or patterned, then ensure they are subtle and not too bold
- Wear a tie that is darker than, and complements your shirt rather than clashes with it
- If wearing a patterned tie, avoid having it in a similar pattern as your shirt
- No floral designs or images/pictures/animated characters of any type
- The length to which your tie should fall is ideally half-way to your belt-buckle; not above, not below
- Wearing a tie-clip or a tie-pin or a tie-bar to keep your tie in place gives you a nice accessory edge
- Watch *YouTube* videos of step-by-step knotting of various styles for neck-ties

SIZZLING HOT 'TIE' TIP –

If you are extra tall or on the shorter side, special length ties are available. Check them out online if you find it difficult to source them in a store

CARRY YOUR **BAG**-GAGE WELL

GUIDELINES FOR MENS' BAGS

- Black or brown, no other colours

- Match your bag colour with your shoes and your belt

- Don't bother too much about matching the right shade of brown for your bag if you are wearing a particular shade of brown shoes. As long as bag and shoes and belt are all in shades of brown, it is fine

- Carry an elegant but spacious bag so it does not look overstuffed even when you load it with all that you need for office

- Make sure you replace the bag if it is looking shabby and worn-out

- Do not carry a backpack if you wish to look truly professional

  (Excellent quality non-leather formal bags are also available)

GUIDELINES FOR **LADIES'** HANDBAGS

- Stick to neutral colours

- Simple design, not too fancy

- Shoulder bags (short straps) are preferable to sling bags

- Avoid separate purses, instead have a spacious bag in which your purse can comfortably fit

- If you are carrying a separate purse, make sure it matches your handbag

- Never carry a backpack to work if you wish to appear professional

JEWELLERY –**LADIES**

While jewellery is an adornment invented and designed to make the wearer look even more beautiful, in office it is advisable to adopt the following guidelines when it comes to wearing jewellery:

- Moderate amount of jewellery
- Simple and elegant, rather than chunky jewellery
- Not more than one pair of earrings
- Small, delicate, dainty earrings are preferred. Avoid dangling earrings
- Either wear a single bracelet or bangles
- If wearing a bracelet, ensure it is not too chunky
- Not more than two or three bangles (If wearing bangles)
- Slim, delicate necklace with elegant and small pendant or locket
- If there are a lot of buttons on your outfit, wear less jewellery
- No more than one ring on each hand

JEWELLERY –**MEN**

The simple guideline here is, avoid any jewellery unless of religious significance or a marriage-ring

LADIES

– Please ensure that your:

- Earrings
- Necklace
- Bracelet/Bangles
- Finger rings
- Buckles on handbag and shoes
- Pen
- Watch.....

.........all match. Either all should be silver-toned or all gold/gold-plated/gold coloured

> ## *All accessories need not have a decorative purpose – some are purely functional*

-CYRUS M. GONDA

CARRY A CLEAN HANDKERCHIEF ON YOU AT ALL TIMES
(AND USE IT WHENEVER NECESSARY)

An article in the *Mumbai Mirror* newspaper dated 20th September, 2014, article titled **MLA WIPES HANDS ON EX-MP's SARI AT FUNCTION**: Bhopal: 'A lawmaker in Madhya Pradesh was caught on camera wiping his hands on a former parliamentarian's sari at a public event on 17th September. Independent legislator Dinesh Rai was on stage at a function in Seoni when he was seen surreptitiously wiping his hands on the sari of former BJP MP Neeta Pateriya, who was apparently oblivious to it. Rai had soiled his hands with oil during the lamp-lighting ceremony for the launch of a crop insurance scheme.'

ACCESSORY
NO-NO'S

AVOID THE FOLLOWING AT WORK
(GUIDELINES FOR MEN AS WELL AS FOR WOMEN)

- **Excess of jewellery**
- **Very high heels**
- **Heavy cologne/perfume**
- **Exercise/gym/sport attire (Avoid these even on Fridays or casual attire days)**
- **Sneakers/Sport shoes**

SOME GENERAL ACCESSORY TIPS
–FOR MEN AND WOMEN ALIKE

" *Elegance is not standing out, but being remembered* "

-GIORGIO ARMANI

- Eye-glasses (if needed):Opt for stylish or classic professional looking frames, not 'funky' ones

- Do not play around with accessories, such as tapping your pen on the table or fiddling with your tie or your watch

- Your cellular phone should have a professional looking sleeve or cover

- Always carry a good quality metal pen and never a plastic one (The metal pen need not be an expensive one)

'WATCH' YOUR WATCH

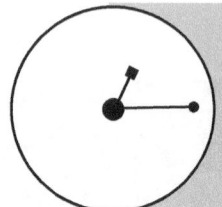

A watch (especially for men, who are denied the opportunity of showcasing bangles and bracelets on their wrists) makes a fantastic fashion accessory and should be selected to showcase your personality to good advantage.

But a watch makes a great accessory item for women as well.

Irrespective of the brand of watch you wear to work (and regardless of how much it cost) the following guidelines should be kept in mind where watches are concerned:

- Select a watch with a professional, rather than a sporty or a funky look
- Sleek, rather than bulky and chunky, demonstrates class and elegance
- Your watch body should always be of metal, and never plastic
- The watch can be in shades of gold or white metal/ steel
- Avoid watches with a lot of buttons and visible functions. The simpler the better
- Your watch should fit your wrist well and not hang loose like a bangle

MATCH YOUR ACCESSORIES
WITH ONE ANOTHER

" *I'm a big believer that accessories can make or break a look* "

-NINA GARCIA

Your accessories should match and never clash with one another. For example, if you are wearing a brown belt with a gold buckle and black shoes and a silver/steel watch, then it is corporate fashion disaster.

Gents should always wear a smart, formal belt with a sleek buckle to work.

Ensure that if your shoes are brown, then so should be your belt, your bag, and also preferably your watch strap. (For kind-hearted souls, there is now an excellent quality of non-leather belts, shoes and bags also available.)

Similarly, your pen, your watch and your belt-buckle should either all be in shades of gold or in shades of silver/steel.

Also cuff-links for men (which you **should** wear once you have climbed the corporate hierarchy) need to match all your other metal accessories as well.

It's not what you spend but how you wear it that counts. The key is often to dress up inexpensive basics with accessories. Something like a beautiful designer bag or belt can make everything else look richer and more luxurious

-CHLOE SEVIGNY

4 GROOMING/ HYGIENE

> **Lots of folk have the looks. But Good Grooming Gives you Genuine Grace**

— CYRUS M. GONDA

On the subjects of grooming, hair care and styling, and make-up, there is no one in India who can equal **OJAS RAJANI** – the leading celebrity make-up artist and hair-stylist. Ojas' list of clientele reads like a veritable who's-who of the Indian celebrity and corporate world.

Some of Ojas' reputed clients from Bollywood include:

- Aishwarya Rai-Bachchan
- Sonam Kapoor
- Deepika Padukone
- Saif Ali Khan
- Arjun Rampal

And a few of Ojas' clients from the Indian corporate world:

- The Dhoot family (owners of Videocon)
- The Vardhan family (owners of Atria Mall, Mumbai)
- Dhirubhai Ambani's granddaughter – Nayantara Kothari
- Chanda Kochar's (of ICICI Bank) daughter's wedding event handled by Ojas
- Rana Kapoor's (of Yes Bank) daughter's wedding event handled by Ojas

And the list can go on and on and on……..

I was fortunate to get an exclusive interview with Ojas for this book, and the expert tips Ojas has shared will be of immense value to us all.

On the vital subject of **HAIR STYLING**, Ojas has the following tips for **MEN**:

> " *People just DON'T take men seriously if they have long hair* "

-OJAS RAJANI

Ojas with Sushmita Sen

Ojas with Deepika Padukone

- Men need to have extremely short, neat, well-groomed` hair-cuts, as these look sleek and stylish

- Short hair-cuts also have the advantage of being easy to maintain and 'no fuss' and make the gentleman appear approachable

- It is recommended that the hair at the back of the head (around the neck region) and the side-burns are regularly shortened and trimmed

- Keep a handy trimmer to trim unruly hair of the beard (if sporting a beard) and also the side-burns and around the neck at the back of the head

- For those with straight hair, get a short cut like the kind Tom Cruise or Vivek Oberoi have, or even an Arjun Kapoor type slightly stylish cut from the front

- For those gents with wavy hair, a very short hair-cut is recommended. A cut for example like Varun Dhawan whose wavy hair is always short and impeccably in place. John Abraham is another excellent example of this style

- For those with greying or receding hair, a dose of *Toppik Hair Fibre Powder* (verify if it suits you medically) is an excellent remedy and acts as a concealer or camouflage for hair greying as well as for balding patches. If needed, you can resort to hair-weaving as a remedy

- Use a scalp cleansing shampoo daily, preferably one which contains zero percent detergent such as *L'Oreal Paris*

- In general, invest in a good quality hair wax or a gel or a serum and use it daily

- If you have a sensitive scalp or receding hair, apply a couple of drops of almond oil on your hair daily

- In office, every couple of hours or so, splash some water on your hair. This also has the dual advantage of refreshing your face and energising you

And the women are not left out.
Ojas has the following tips for

HAIR CARE FOR WOMEN

in the corporate world:

- Hair should never be falling over the face and should always be pushed back neatly into a bun or a pony-tail

- Open hair is a distraction and those women who leave their long hair open in a corporate environment run the risk of not being taken seriously

- A great example of a neat corporate hairstyle would be that of Bipasha Basu in the movie 'Corporate'

- For those women with a lean face, a slick pony-tail with or without a hair-band or a neat 'updo' or a chignon would work wonders

- For those women with a broader face, a blunt hair-cut looks good. As an example of a 'blunt' cut, see the air-hostesses of *IndiGo Airlines*, who either have their hair cut in a 'blunt' cut or who wear a 'blunt-cut' wig. This makes them look really chic, modern and stylish

- For those women with wavy hair, they should definitely not leave their hair open. They should use an anti-frizz serum daily and ensure their hair is kept pushed back in a bun or a pony-tail or an 'updo.' Do not keep your hair cut short and leave it open if it is wavy as it would look frizzy and undone

- If hair is greying, you could colour it if you feel the need or leave it as it is as grey hair looks distinguished

- For women with receding hair, ideally get your hair cut in a lot of layers and use in-built bouffant clips. There are also a lot of beautiful hair-extensions available in the market which would be of good use

OJAS provides expert corporate **make-up** tips for women:

- Women at work should use very matt and very clean make-up

- Keeping the Indian climate in mind, use a compact (powder) foundation daily and also a good sun-screen

- Use lip-balm or lipstick in a soft colour

- Make use of a *kaajal* pencil for the eyes in either black or brown according to personal taste

- Do not apply extra blush or eye-shadow as these can be a big distraction at work

- For nails, use either bold red nail-polish or a classic French manicure (white-tipped)

For both men and for women, **OJAS** advises no gum chewing, but do use a mouth wash frequently.

In fact, you should always have the following with you at work and use when needed:

- Deodorant
- Mouth wash/Breath freshener spray
- Hand sanitiser
- Cooling aftershave for men/Light perfume for women

And for **men** alone, Ojas advises:

- Nails to be always trimmed short and regularly cleaned
- Wearing a vest under the shirt else the shirt looks soiled when perspiration occurs. Vests which can tuck in your stomach when worn are also now available

And lastly, Ojas has some advice for **women** on the **jewellery** suitable for office wear:

- Small studs as earrings are the best
- No hanging earrings
- No heavy necklaces or large brooches
- A neat, sleek watch

Thank you, Ojas. *The readers will definitely benefit from your expert grooming inputs.*

AN----------------
INTERESTING
-------------FACT

O ver a period of time, it has been noted that **98%** of the men on the *Forbes 100 List of Richest Men*.....are......**clean-shaven**

Some of the iconic global corporate and business tycoons who were/are clean shaven are:

- **Henry Ford**

- **Sam Walton**

- **Jack Welch**

- **Bill Gates**

- **Ratan Tata**

A clean-shaven look is always preferable.

If in case you are sporting a moustache or a beard, ensure it is well trimmed and does not resemble a lawn which has not been mowed for months.

"Good grooming is integral and impeccable style is a must. If you don't look the part, no one will want to give you time or money"

-DAYMOND JOHN

WHAT GETS NOTICED
FIRST>>>>>

When a man is noticed in a corporate setting by another individual, normally what is observed first in that man's appearance and grooming by the other is (**in order of priority**):

- **Shoes** (polished, heel not worn out)

- **Sleeve cuffs** (well ironed, not stained)

- **Belt** (not scratched or worn out, buckle shining)

- **Watch** (elegant and sophisticated)

- **Pen** (metal body, sleek look)

- **Bag** (corporate design, not scratched or worn out)

- **Hair** (short and neatly trimmed)

- **Shave** (clean shaven, if keeping moustache or beard ensure well trimmed)

Now that you know what others look for in you first, you can start scoring full marks in these vital areas of grooming and appearance and start off your business relationship/meeting on a good note.

After all, as is said:

WELL BEGUN IS HALF DONE

TAKE CARE :
EVERYTHING
ABOUT YOU IS BEING
NOTICED AND EVALUATED

Following is an extract from an article titled:

'Watch how you touch up. Even a chipped nail paint can cost a job' which appeared in the *Times of India* newspaper, Mumbai edition, dated 1st October, 2012.

(The article is based on a piece written by **Ben Spencer** for the Daily Mail, U.K.):

'......Interviewers make all sorts of snap judgements about a candidate's character based solely on their grooming regime, according to a new survey of British bosses. In a survey of 2,000 executives by a UK based fashion retailer, one in four bosses said that chipped nail varnish quickly takes the shine off an applicant's chances, as it makes them appear nervous or unprepared.

A fifth of managers see split hair ends as a sign of laziness, and one in six said smudged mascara made them fear hiring a 'party animal' who would be quick to escape the office for a bar, the Daily Mail reported. A deep tan leads bosses to the conclusion that a candidate would gladly abandon their duties for the pleasures of a beach-break, while bright red lipstick, heavily pencilled eyebrows and overpowering perfume are considered indicative of an overconfident and cocky personality.

The common scenario of lipstick smudged onto teeth apparently suggests carelessness, while foundation that hasn't been blended properly is seen to highlight a lack of attention to detail.

Even going for a natural look isn't without risks, as certain bosses believe the absence of mascara indicates an emotional wreck who worries that it would all be cried off within hours. An immaculately made up face makes some recruiters fear this candidate means business and will be snapping at their heels for the next promotion.'

As you can see, **EVERYTHING** you wear or use to adorn yourself can be viewed critically by people who matter, so take extra care not to falter in even a single grooming and attire area which could cost you a coveted job/promotion/sale/ business deal.

AIM TO LOOK YOUR BEST AT **ALL** TIMES

Madame de Pompadour, the mistress of Louis XV of France, and an important political figure in her own right, was always extremely particular and alert as regards her personal grooming – a great role model for all to follow.

In 1764, as she lay dying, she summoned her strength, called out to God, "Please wait a second," and dabbed her cheeks with rouge, preparing herself for her final journey.

ALWAYS TAKE PRIDE IN YOUR APPEARANCE

In 2010, thirty-three miners in Chile, trapped underground for many weeks in a mine, were gradually brought out to safety.

As these traumatised men were preparing to leave their temporary enforced underground home and breathe fresh air once more, they requested for **clean socks**, **shampoo**, and **shoe polish** before they emerged on solid ground.

The miners wanted their hair free of dust and their shoes to shine when they faced their family and friends again.

GOOD GROOMING
IS A PACKAGE DEAL

Good grooming and good manners are inseparable.

Which is why the better Business Schools insist that their students attend college in formal outfits daily.

Automatically, when a gentleman is dressed in formal clothes, he shaves every day and ensures his shoes are polished before he leaves home.

This also has an impact on his behaviour and makes him behave like a gentleman should.

You simply **CANNOT** wear a formal outfit and then leave home unshaven and with casual shoes and behave shabbily.

There is much to support the view that it is clothes that wear us and not we them; we may make them take the mould of our physical arm or breast, but they would mould our hearts, our brains, our tongues to their liking

-VIRGINIA WOOLF

GOOD GROOMING
FORMS A LIFE-LONG HABIT
WHICH WILL SERVE YOU WELL

It is said that if a person practices an activity conscientiously and dedicatedly, daily for a period of three weeks, then that activity becomes a life-long habit with that person.

This is true in the case of good grooming as well.

Observe a career officer from the defence services. Even on their day-off, while on vacation, or even after they have retired from the armed forces, you will always find them clean-shaven (or with moustache/beard well-trimmed), their shoes shining, their hair in place, their clothes well-ironed.

They take **PRIDE** in their appearance. And this is the result of rigorous training in grooming habits inculcated during the early days when they were raw recruits.

You, too, can practice the tips provided throughout this book for a period of twenty-one continuous days and develop a habit which will serve you well throughout your professional career and even after.

GROOM YOURSELF EXTRA-CAREFULLY
FOR SPECIAL OCCASIONS

Your grooming, including your hair, needs to be appropriately trimmed as the occasion demands.

On 8th October, 2014, the Indian cricketing legend, Sachin Tendulkar (who has been given the honorary rank of Group Captain of the Indian Air Force), attended an Air Force Day Parade at the Hindon Air Force station in Ghaziabad, adorned in his Group Captain uniform complete with officer's cap.

A letter by reader T.R. Ramaswami in the 'Letters' column of the *Afternoon Despatch & Courier* newspaper (Mumbai edition) dated 9th October, 2014 read as follows:

'A **Disgrace To Uniform'** – 'Did you see Group Captain (Honorary) Sachin Tendulkar in uniform at a recent air show? What a disgrace! I thought it was some lady air force officer, with his hair sticking out like a sore thumb..... Perhaps the air force should give him some sartorial (dressing) lessons.'

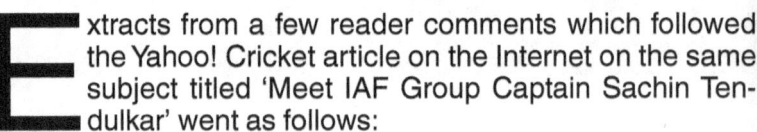

E xtracts from a few reader comments which followed the Yahoo! Cricket article on the Internet on the same subject titled 'Meet IAF Group Captain Sachin Tendulkar' went as follows:

- 'I was in the NCC at college. I cut my hair military style when the rest of my classmates (non-NCC) used to have long hair. Sachin doesn't even want to lose a little hair to be worthy of the uniform he is wearing and the honor bestowed on him by our hero worshipping government....'

- 'Disgrace to the Air Force uniform and to the Rank. He should learn how to crop his hair in uniform and be taught how to salute. A total disgrace.....'

- 'He cannot salute properly, he does not trim his hair, he did not remove ornaments on his right hand.....'

- 'If the country considers him to be of such importance, then Sachin should have considered the strict discipline of the air force and trimmed his hair before going into this ceremony....'

LADIES,
WHILE MAKE-UP IS
ESSENTIAL,
DON'T OVERDO IT

Hyacinthe **Rigaud**, the 18th century French painter, was painting the portrait of a lady who had applied extremely bright and heavy make-up.

While the portrait was being painted, she complained to Rigaud that the colours he had used to portray her face on the painting were too bright and gaudy.

Rigaud courteously replied, "We both buy our colours at the same shop, madame."

GROOMING MATTERS
– IT MATTERS A GREAT DEAL

A study conducted on hiring managers in Illinois, U.S.A., by the consumer giant **Procter & Gamble** in 2011 found that **men who are well-groomed are more likely to get and retain their jobs.**

Six out of ten hiring managers surveyed in the study said that **well-groomed candidates were more likely to climb up the corporate hierarchy faster** than those who do not keep themselves well-groomed.

Another survey finding – 78 percent of the hiring managers surveyed believed that **well-groomed candidates have more self-confidence.**

And based on certain Bureau of Labor statistics in the Illinois region, Procter & Gamble believes that **making a good first impression can be a critical factor in getting hired and/ or keeping a job in a tough job market.**

The research findings mentioned above appear on the site **cosmeticsdesign.com** under the header '**P&G study finds that appearance matters in employment**' and was authored by Andrew McDougall.

Well, what holds true for hiring managers in Illinois, U.S.A., apparently would hold good for most hiring managers across the globe, wouldn't it?

A ccording to a survey conducted by **CareerBuild-er.com** in 2011,conducted on over 2,800 employers, there are **specific grooming and hygiene related reasons why employers would not offer an employee a job promotion**.

Based on the results of the survey, the following are the determined **reasons related to workplace grooming that may cause an employer not to promote a worker**.

The percentage mentioned against the factor is the percentage of employers surveyed who stressed on that particular factor as being a specifically negative one, as far as they were concerned:

• Piercings	**37 percent**
• Having bad breath	**34 percent**
• Visible tattoo	**31 percent**
• Wearing wrinkled/unironed clothes	**31 percent**
• Untidy and messy hair	**29 percent**
• Dressing too casually	**28 percent**
• Excessive perfume or cologne	**26 percent**
• Messy work-station or cubicle	**19 percent**
• Having chewed fingernails	**10 percent**

A similar relationship could very well exist between salespersons/service persons/front-end executives and the success rate of their relationships with their colleagues, customers and clients.

Now that you know which are the grooming-related factors that '**turn people off**' you can groom yourself accordingly to '**turn them on**' and secure that job/promotion/sale.

ESSENTIAL HYGIENE / GROOMING TIPS
(FOR MEN AS WELL AS FOR WOMEN)

- Always wash hands and face after every meal

- Avoid strong-smelling foods while at work

- Brush your teeth in the morning as well as at night

- Use a deodorant or anti-perspirant when needed

- Do apply cologne or perfume, but not one with a very strong or overpowering fragrance

- If needed, consider getting your teeth whitened and done up cosmetically for a great smile. It is a worthwhile investment as white, even teeth are one of the first things we tend to appreciate in the people we meet

(I can personally recommend my dentists – Dr. Merwaan-Farog (Ahura Dental Clinic) in South Mumbai and Dr. Umesh Trivedi in Bandra (West), Mumbai – they are both simply brilliant at their work, honest and reasonable as well)

"*A genuine smile comes from the heart, but a healthy smile needs good dental care*"

-WAYNE CHIRISA

HYGIENE / GROOMING TIPS
–MEN

- Men – Shave **DAILY** – no stubble should be visible if you are sporting a clean-shaven look

- Men – Change your socks daily. Apply talcum powder on feet if necessary

- Nose/ear hair to be clipped if and when required

A FUNNY FACT –

Because of his poor personal hygiene in his earlier days, Steve Jobs was asked to work the night shift when employed with *Atari*, so he would be around fewer people.

HYGIENE / GROOMING TIPS
–WOMEN

- Check that nail polish not chipped or shabbily applied

- Hair neatly done-up, irrespective of hairstyle adopted

- Lipstick not smeared

- Avoid very long nails

- No excessive make-up

SIZZLING HOT
'HYGIENE' TIP

ALWAYS CARRY WITH YOU OR IN YOUR BAG:

- Hand sanitiser

- Breath freshener spray

- Clean handkerchief

- Small bottle of cologne, aftershave for men / perfume for women

- Comb

5 POWER DRESSING

"*Power dressing is about learning to present yourself in the most dramatic way. It's about dressing in a manner that projects importance or success*"

-ALAN FLUSSER
(owner of a New York custom-clothing shop for men)

D on't assume that just because the U.S.A. has an informal culture, that even the senior executives there dress and speak casually in a professional environment.

In fact, at 'high-power meetings' in Corporate Headquarters of the leading Fortune 500 companies (most of which are based in the U.S.A.), it is power-dressing which works – **charcoal colour suit**, **red tie**, **white shirt**, **gleaming black shoes**.

Formal attire in a formal environment is always expected and appreciated. If you wish to positively stand out, you can't ignore this.

Not too many years ago, everyone dressed formally and conservatively.

See old Charlie Chaplin movies.

See real-life photographs of the Mafia leaders and their henchmen; they dressed as well as senior executives did.

In those days, even thieves and tramps wore a lie and a hat, though they could hardly afford a bite to eat. Today, people deliberately buy ripped and torn designer jeans for Rs. 25,000 and wear them to receptions in a 5-Star environment.

The single most important rule for 'Power-Dressing' is –

'DRESS CONSERVATIVELY'

THE BEST-DRESSED CEOs LIST

On the Internet you can find images of 'America's Best Dressed CEOs.'

Viewing them, you could find inspiration for the days when **YOU** need to be 'dressed-at-your-best.'

Recent entrants on this 'Powerful' list include:

MEN

- Robert A. Iger of the Walt Disney Co.

- Antonio Reid of Epic Records

- James Dimon of J.P. Morgan Chase & Co.

LADIES

- Ellen Kullman of DuPont

- Oprah Winfrey of OWN Network

- Desiree Rogers of Johnson Publishing Co.

Meher Castelino is a fashion icon and legend. She

was elected the **first ever Miss India** in 1964 by *Femina* and she has **pioneered the concept of fashion journalism in India**. She has been labelled '**an inspiration for many and an asset for the country**.'

Meher is:

- A leading international fashion consultant

- A lecturer at several premium Indian fashion institutes

- The official post-show writer for fashion weeks in India

 **Meher was kind enough to grant me an exclusive interview for this book and has provided many invaluable tips for 'POWER DRESSING' for gents as well as for ladies across the spectrum of attire and accessories. A concentrated and condensed version of her expert inputs follows:**

" *Make a great first impression they say and it's the most lasting one. This probably holds good especially for high-powered jet-legging corporate honchos and their female counterparts. Since big business means big bucks and involves lots of wheeling and dealing, therefore it is that look of authority and competence that one's sartorial preferences exude which play a great role in corporate success* "

-MEHER CASTELINO

Do's and Don'ts
for 'Power Business Wear'
–suggested by Meher Castelino

For Him

1. A good suit is worth its weight in gold, so invest in one wisely

2. Do not leave the double-breasted jacket undone. It looks tacky for an executive

3. Ensure your shirts are crisp and in Oxford, Chambray or Cambric. Keep the silks and satins out of the boardroom

4. Don't fill up the pockets of your business suit. The briefcase is meant for holding things

5. Pick the right suit fabric that works well for you. Select from houndstooth, chalk-stripe, herringbone, pin-stripe or birdseye

6. Keep the business tie toned down and subtle yet rich and ensure that the knot hides the collar band and the tip touches the waistband of the trouser

7. Shirts with bold patterns must be accompanied with solid coloured ties

8. Don't be 'hep' by wearing trainers with the suit. Lace-up shoes are still the correct formal choice

9. Pocket squares (for very formal attire) should be visible by a few centimetres from the top of the breast pocket in the suit jacket

----

WHAT IS A
'POCKET SQUARE?'

(The following explanation of a pocket square is from 'The Encyclopedia Of Men's Clothes')

'The pocket handkerchief or pocket square, as most quality men's stores call it, is a silk, linen or cotton fabric that is usually from 13 to 18 inches square.

It is square in shape as required by a 1785 Royal French Decree.

It's a fashion accessory for adding another element of style to enhance your look and it's **the only reason we have breast pockets** on our suits and sport coats. The pocket square is purely decorative.'

For Her

1. A couple of good all-purpose jackets in a neutral colour should be an integral part of your business wardrobe. These can be then dressed up or down

2. Blouses or shirts in small or medium prints or solid colours work well for the office

3. Have a collection of pants and skirts of neutral colours like black, white, beige, brown, ivory and navy to mix and match

4. For ethnic wear, cotton or blended *sarees* work best for the office. They go well with matching elbow-sleeves blouses. Keep the halters and bikini cholis for the party circuit

5. Wear pearls or a simple gold chain and small earrings, a single bangle and not a dozen as they will get noisy

6. A smart tunic/*kameeze* with *salwars* or *churidars* works well for a 9 to 5 day

7. Keep the length of the dress or the skirt at the knees. Minis are tiresome when rushing from one meeting to another

8. Crisp cotton or jute blends for *sarees* work well through the busy day

9. Keep footwear comfortable and stylish. Avoid spindly stilettos

Thanks a ton, Meher. These expert tips for ladies and gents will surely be of great use to the readers.

SOME GENERAL TIPS FOR
'POWER DRESSING'

f you are already in the upper rungs of the corporate ladder, or even as a relative junior, for that 'special' meeting when you want to exude power and authority, the following tips would make you appear to be a key decision-maker.

- Rich colours and shades are the key to power dressing. As an example, if you select to wear a red tie, select a deep, rich shade of red

- Suits look their most powerful best in deep charcoal or rich midnight-blue (avoid jet-black)

- A simple rule of thumb for men – the darker the colour, the higher the apparent authority

- Women could spend a little extra on their skirt and jacket and also on their shoes and hand-bag. These are the items of attire and accessory which are immediately noticed on women

- Women should avoid wearing soft or light fabrics which do not 'sit well' on the figure

- Also, when you put your photo profiles on professional social media sites such as *LinkedIn*, show yourself at your formal best

SIZZLING HOT 'POWER DRESSING' TIP –

If possible, get your best outfits tailored for you rather than buy them 'off-the-shelf' as no body or figure is perfect

'POWER DRESSING'
LITERALLY OPENS ALL DOORS FOR THE WEARER

With the right attire and superior grooming automatically comes confidence. There is the recent story of a couple, **Michaele and Tareq Salahi**, though not invitees, managed to attend an exclusive dinner hosted by President Barrack Obama in honour of Indian Prime Minister Manmohan Singh.

The couple managed to get through two security checkpoints without even having an invite, as they had attired themselves like royalty.

Michaele spent seven hours in a salon getting ready for the event, and wore expensive designer jewellery and a gold-embroidered red Indian-style dress to the event.

They mingled with the VIPs present at the event and even managed to get photos taken alongside most of the legitimate guests.

The *Washington Post* newspaper later surmised that the Salahis were allowed to enter without an invite because they **'looked the part.'**

This is not to say that you should misuse 'power dressing' for the wrong reasons. **Rather, this example should be taken in positive light as it gives you an insight as to how seriously you are taken when you 'dress the part.'**

6 FRIDAY DRESSING
Smart Casuals

People used to talk about dressing more casually in the office, but that hasn't really worked out. People need to look a certain way to command authority

-GRAEME BLACK
(HEAD DESIGNER, FERRAGAMO'S)

Since the ultimate objective of **ALL** corporate dressing (including Casual Dressing/Friday Dressing) is to create a positive impact on those who matter through the care you have taken on your external appearance, it is important to bear in mind while dressing 'casually' for work that even your casual business attire should demonstrate that **YOU MEAN BUSINESS**.

If you still believe that 'Friday Dressing' permits you to indulge yourself for that 'one day a week' in sloppy attire, please read the **Dilbert** book titled –

'CASUAL DAY HAS GONE TOO FAR'

THANK GOD IT'S FRIDAY

As previously mentioned, there is a strong relationship between the way you dress and the way you behave.

Jackson Lewis, a firm that specialises in human resource related issues, interviewed over a thousand human resource executives who had implemented a **casual dress policy** in their organisations.

These organisations reported a **thirty percent increase in flirtatious and other unprofessional behaviour after the casual dress policies were implemented.**

When you dress in a professional manner, your behaviour sub-consciously shifts forward to professional gear to match the way you look, and vice-versa.

DRESSING DOWN
–FRIDAY DRESSING

The following is an extract from the classic work: *How To Be A Gentleman – A Timely Guide To Timeless Manners*, authored by John Bridges:

I n some office environments, "Casual Fridays" are a standing tradition, the one day a week when the office dress code eases up and employees are permitted (and even encouraged) to dress more informally, as a means of acknowledging the onset of the impending weekend.

When a gentleman starts work at a new office, however, he does not take it for granted that every week closes with a "casual" day. Unless he is told otherwise, he comes to work on Friday dressed precisely the way he dresses for any other work day.

Even if his office does subscribe to a "Casual Fridays" policy, a gentleman still dresses neatly and professionally.

He may choose to wear chinos, a polo shirt, or a sports shirt with a blazer, and loafers.

Unless, over the course of time, he observes co-workers wearing jeans, he does not even think of doing so.'

f your organisation has a policy of **FRIDAY DRESSING / CASUAL DRESSING**, ladies as well as gents should keep in mind the following:

Remember, the key word is **SMART** casual.

AVOID (even for 'Friday Dressing')

- Collarless shirts
- Denims
- Jeans
- Sleeveless attire
- Sandals

**WEAR**
- Socks with your shoes

- A belt in pant loops if your shirt is tucked in and pant loops are visible

Men take care, if you happen to dress too casually, you may possibly omit to shave as well.

TIPS FOR 'FRIDAY DRESSING' / CASUAL DRESSING FOR MEN

AVOID (TOP)

- Round-necked tee-shirts
- Track-suit jackets

PERMITTED (TOP)

- Short-sleeved shirt (not very gaudy patterns)
- Polo-necked top
- Casual blazer
- Collared tee-shirts

AVOID (BOTTOM)

- Cargo pants
- Jeans
- Shorts
- Linen pants

PERMIITTED (BOTTOM)

- Corduroys
- Chinos
- Cotton trousers

TIPS FOR 'FRIDAY DRESSING' / CASUAL DRESSING FOR WOMEN

AVOID (TOP)

- Tank tops
- Sleeveless tops
- See-through tops

PERMITTED (TOP)

- Casual blazer
- Dresses that cover the shoulder
- Short-sleeved shirt
- Polo-necked top
- Sweater

AVOID (BOTTOM)

- Leggings
- Shorts
- Cargo pants
- Jeans

PERMITTED (BOTTOM)

- Chinos
- Cotton trousers
- Capris
- Khakis

And when it comes to
FOOTWEAR FOR FRIDAYS:

For **GENTS**.........Loafers are fine....

But **NO**

- Sandals
- Sport shoes
- Hiking boots

And for **LADIES**......Flat/low-heeled shoes would do well....

But again..... **NO**

- Sport shoes
- Sandals
- Boots

A s promised earlier in this book, **Ashley Rebello** (the man with the magic fashion touch), is back with his unique offerings of colour schemes and choice of attire to make your 'Friday at Work' perfect in every way.

" Friday Dressing has a lot to do with your individual personality that should reflect through your clothes in a semi-formal way "

-ASHLEY REBELLO

For **MEN**, Ashley recommends a few of his personal favourites:

- Chino pants go well with Polo tee-shirts

- Khaki pants with an ink-blue shirt

- Brown / beige corduroys with half-sleeve fitted baby-pink / maroon shirts

- For shoes, slip-ons / loafers

- A sling-bag is fine for Friday

For **LADIES' FRIDAY WESTERN WEAR,**
Ashley suggests:

- A pair of grey Palazzo pants with a nice teal-coloured fitted round-neck tee-shirt

- A flared box-pleated skirt (either knee-length or full-length) in a solid colour like an emerald-green and a Portofino (fitted) shirt

And for **LADIES' FRIDAY INDIAN WEAR**, Ashley recommends:

- A good *kurti* with a pair of fitted trousers

Lastly, Ashley advises, accessories should always be minimal even on Fridays, as you are ultimately in a corporate environment.

7 BODY LANGUAGE

> ## "The best thing you can wear is self confidence"

-AULIQ LEE

While clothes and accessories may be your 'second skin,' your 'first skin' – the body you were born with, is all important when it comes to projecting a positive self-image.

It makes little sense to invest in the best attire and accessories, be impeccably groomed and freshly-fragrant, and then spoil it all by not demonstrating the right body language.

Since this is primarily a book on attire and grooming, I will not go into depth on the subject of body language, but provide the basic tips which will ensure that your effort in selecting the right attire and accessories does not go in vain.

The very first thing to remember in projecting a positive impression through body language is your facial expression – let it not be grumpy but cheerful and welcoming.

" Good humour is one of the best articles of dress one can wear in society "

-WILLIAM MAKEPEACE THACKERAY

THE RELATIONSHIP BETWEEN
YOUR SHOES AND YOUR
BODY LANGUAGE

For your body language to be comfortable, it is very important that your shoes fit you well and do not 'pinch' you anywhere nor are too tight.

The body rests on the feet, and if your feet are not comfortable in your shoes, your body language will appear strained and weak.

Ensure when you select footwear (ladies as well as gents) that it not only looks elegant but also feels comfortable.

" A shoe is not only a design, but it is part of your body language, the way you walk. The way you're going to move is quite dictated by your shoes "

-CHRISTIAN LOUBOUTIN

Some tips to ensure you attract people towards you through the positive power of body language:

- Stand erect, but not stiff, with your weight equally distributed on both legs, both legs about five inches apart

- Keep your chin up, but not so high that it faces the sky

- Keep your hands loosely by your sides most of the time while standing

- Don't sway back and forth

- Don't lean backward, forward or sideways on any piece of furniture

- Don't play with keys or loose change in your pockets

- When pointing towards something, point with an open palm facing the object, not a closed fist with just the index finger pointing

- Don't stand with your hands placed on your hips

- Allow at least one and a half feet space between you and the other person you are speaking or interacting with. This distance defines a person's personal space which should not be crossed, else it makes the other person feel uncomfortable

And last, but not the least, remember:

"*Of all the things you wear, your expression is the most important*"

-Unknown

AUTHOR PROFILE

CYRUS M GONDA

Cyrus enjoys and specialises in conducting training workshops and providing consultancy in the following areas, all of which are based on trademarked models developed/co-developed by him:

- Etiquette and soft skill development (Based on the 'E.T.I.Q.U.E.T.T.E. Model ™')

- 5 Star Leadership (Based on the trademarked '5 V Model ™')

- Power Listening (Based on the trademarked 'Power Of Listening Model ™')

- Sales and Customer Relationship Excellence (Based on the trademarked 'Be a Super Salesperson Model ™')

- Strategy Formulation and Implementation (A trademarked model developed)

- High Performance Presentation Skills (A trademarked model developed)

- Strategic Communication Skills (A trademarked model developed)

Cyrus is uniquely qualified to facilitate workshops on Corporate Business Etiquette. He is:

- A rank holder in Hotel Management from the Sophia Polytechnic, Mumbai

- A rank holder MBA in Human Resources from NMIMS, Mumbai University

- He is a qualified MENSA International life member and an acknowledged thought leader in the areas of leadership, communication and management, and is a spontaneous, entertaining and enlightening speaker

- He has secured the A1 Grade in the third and highest level of Business English Communication from Cambridge

- Has rich experience in leading multinational organisations in the service as well as in the manufacturing sector, in operational as well as administrative positions, in India and overseas

- He Is a communicator and logician par excellence. His workshops are filled with interesting business anecdotes, of which he has a memorable wealth at his disposal for every occasion

- Has authored many best-selling books on customer service excellence and leadership

Cyrus currently is:

- The Head of Department - Strategic Communication, at Rizvi Management Institutes, Mumbai

- Jt. Managing Director of the leadership and management consultancy firm - Brains Trust India

- A visiting faculty at leading management institutes and hotel management institutes

- Faculty at the National Institute of Event Management

- Trainer for the air hostess and purser course at IITC, India's premier and largest institute for IATA students

- Certified as faculty by Regency University of TAFE, South Australia, for hospitality, leisure and food studies

- Life Member of the Bombay Management Association

- Fellow Member of the Film Writer's Association

A few of the organisations for which Cyrus has conducted training workshops include:

- Abbott India Ltd.
- Ashok Piramal Group
- BASF
- Bharat Petroleum (BPCL)
- Burgmann India
- Central Depository Services Limited (CDSL)
- Chr. Hansen India
- Godrej & Boyce
- HDFC Bank
- Hindustan Unilever (HUL)
- Indian Navy
- Lawrence & Mayo
- Lions Club
- Mahindra
- TajSATS (Taj Mahal Hotel and Singapore Airlines Terminal Services joint-venture)
- Tata Motors
- Tata VSNL
- Triumph lingerie
- Westside retail

Cyrus can be contacted for facilitating training workshops, providing consultancy inputs and for short speaking assignments on various subjects at:

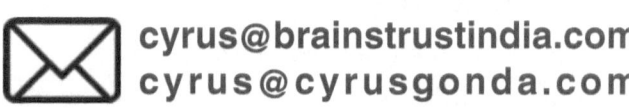 **cyrus@brainstrustindia.com**
cyrus@cyrusgonda.com